I'M FUN, TOO!

Jonathan Fenske

Scholastic Inc.

To Pendy, Coco, and Lulu, the pieces that make the set complete!

ISBN 978-1-338-32561-4

10 9 8 7 6 5 4 3 2 1   18 19 20 21 22

Printed in the U.S.A.   40

First edition 2018

Yep. Two dots and one line.
That's all I get.

happy

sad

mad

scared

Even when it REALLY HURTS.

Hmmmph. Not the FUN, NEW guys.

happy

sad

mad

scared

They LAUGH!

They SHOUT!

They SING!

I USED to have the best BIKE on the block.

Not anymore.

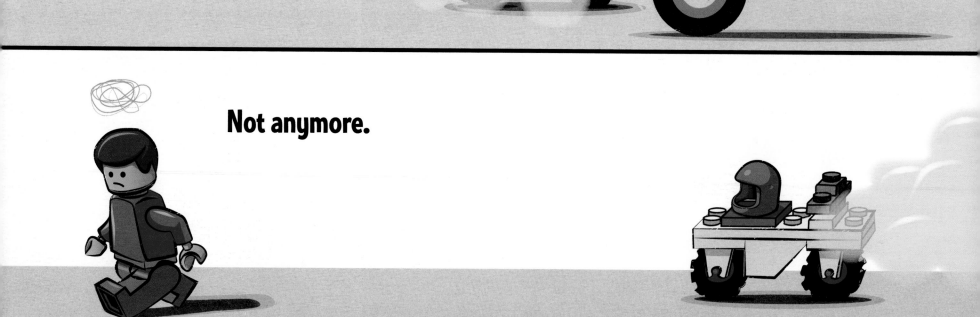

Let's face it. If we were ice cream . . .

. . . those guys would be SUPER-DUPER CHUNKY HAPPY BIRTHDAY BLAST.

And I would be VANILLA.

It would be so fun to have such a SUNNY SMILE.
But this suit is driving me BANANAS.

But I'm like a blank sheet of paper!

I'm like an empty canvas!

I can be whomever I WANT to be!

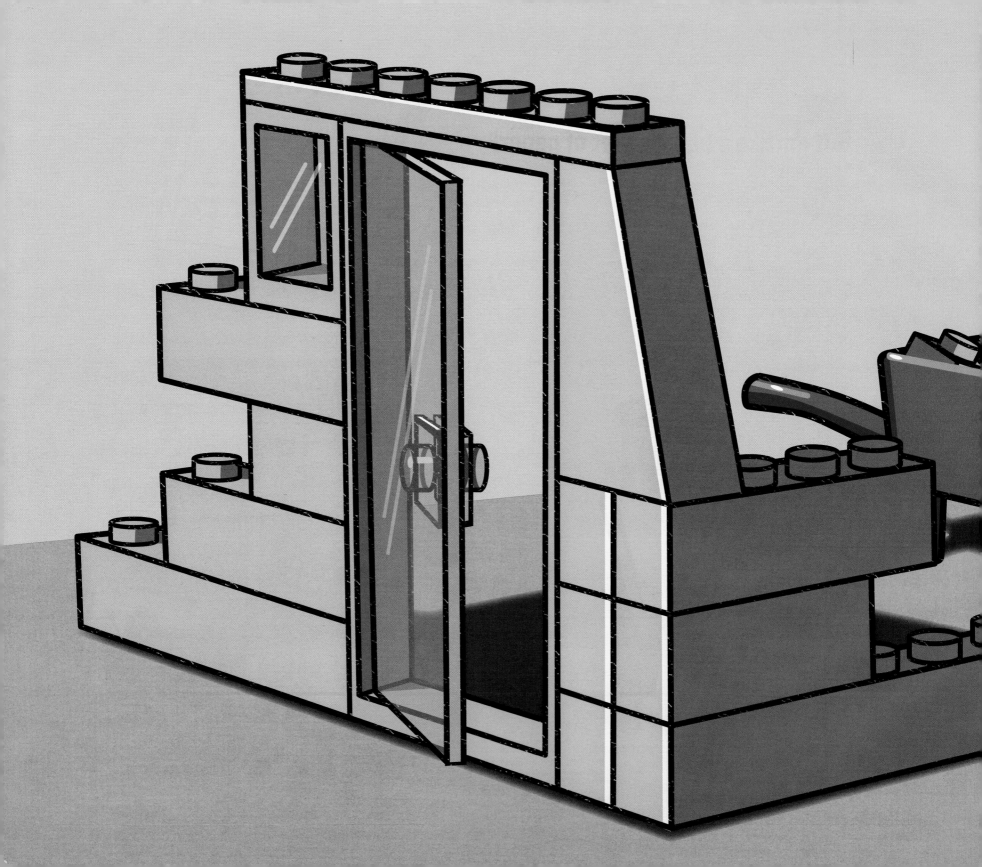

Give me a SWORD and I'll save the day!

Give me a **ROCKET**
and I'll reach the stars!